A LE

TO JA

A LETTER
TO JABEZ

BY NEAL E. SNIDER

Augsburg Books
MINNEAPOLIS

A LETTER TO JABEZ
Response to a Prayer

Large-quantity purchases or custom editions of this book are available at a discount from the publisher. For more information, contact the sales department at Augsburg Fortress, Publishers, 1-800-328-4648, or write to: Sales Director, Augsburg Fortress, Publishers, P.O. Box 1209, Minneapolis, MN 55440-1209.

Unless indicated otherwise, scripture quotations are from the Revised Standard Version of the Bible, copyright © 1946, 1952, 1971 by the Division of Christian Education of the National Council of the Churches of Christ in the USA. Used by permission.

Scripture quotations marked NKJV are taken from The New King James Version, copyright © 1979, 1980, 1982 Thomas Nelson, Inc. Used by permission. All rights reserved.

ISBN 0-8066-4647-0

Cover design by Marti Naughton
Book design by Michelle L. N. Cook

The paper used in this publication meets the minimum requirements of American National Standard for Information Sciences—Permanence of Paper for Printed Library Materials, ANSI Z329.48-1984. ∞ ™

Manufactured in the U.S.A.

08   07   06   05   04   1   2   3   4   5   6   7   8   9   10

This book is dedicated to my grandchildren:

Sandra Morrow

Weston Morrow

Quinn Morrow

Elise Rodriguez

Marc Rodriguez

CONTENTS

Now Jabez was more honorable than his brothers, and his mother called his name Jabez, saying, "Because I bore him in pain."

And Jabez called on the God of Israel saying, "Oh that You would bless me indeed, and enlarge my territory, that Your hand would be with me, and that You would keep me from evil, that I may not cause pain!" So God granted him what he requested.

(1 Chronicles 4:9-10 NKJV)

INTRODUCTION

January 2004
Mr. Jabez
Wherever you are

Dear Mr. Jabez:

I read your prayer. I know very little about you, but that's okay; you know even less about me.

The person who wrote about your prayer, recorded in our Bible, didn't say where you lived, nor when you lived, nor even who your father was. He wrote a very extensive genealogy, but just stuck the story about your prayer into his genealogy without saying how you fit there. Because of where he placed your story I have to guess that you probably lived a few generations after Abraham, Isaac, and Jacob—perhaps about 1500 B.C. That's still a couple hundred years before Moses.

I'm so pleased that God heard your prayer and granted what you asked. I find great joy in celebrating the blessings that God grants to others. Please don't misunderstand me. I do not mean that others have been blessed by God and I have not. Nothing could be further from the truth. This I share with you: God has blessed both of us in super abundance.

I find added delight in knowing that you, who lived about thirty-five hundred years before me, prayed to the same God as I. That gives us some kind of a kinship. Oh, it's more than just the fatherhood of God and the brotherhood of man that unites us. I guess that there is some truth in that cliché, but our kinship is closer than that vague truism. We are united in a bond that reaches back several generations before you, to Abraham, through whom God made a covenant with humanity. That bond reaches forward from you to me through Jesus.

Oh, I forgot. You didn't know anything about Jesus. He didn't arrive on the scene until about fifteen hundred years after you "slept with your fathers." Surely you have heard a great deal about him during the past two thousand years. He is the one through whom God fulfilled the promise to Abraham and his descendants—the promise that God would bless all humanity.

I fear that I am digressing a bit, but I did want to establish our kinship, and tell you how pleased I am that you were blessed by God.

I have wondered how your prayer found its way into our Bible. The word *Bible* may not be familiar to you since in your day there was no Bible, only the telling of the story of God's mighty acts among his people from generation to generation. Those "mighty acts," most of which occurred after your day, have been written and recorded for all succeeding generations. That record we call our Bible. That's not a very exciting title because *Bible* simply means "book."

But how did your prayer ever find its way into our Bible? Neither you nor I know the name of the person who included it in the story. We only know the author of that part of our Bible as The Chronicler. We have divided the chronicles that he recorded into two parts. We call them First Chronicles and Second Chronicles. It's really one continuous story, but was too long to be contained on one scroll when it was originally written. Consequently, when two scrolls were required to hold all his writing, one scroll was called First Chronicles and the second scroll Second Chronicles. Your prayer is contained in the fourth chapter and the tenth verse of First Chronicles. (The chapters and verses were not part of The Chronicler's writings. Only less than a thousand years ago someone divided the different writings of the Bible into chapters and verses for easier citation).

The Chronicler lived and wrote more than a thousand years after your time. How did he know about your prayer? You must have related it to somebody, and it was passed down through the generations until The Chronicler recorded it with the rest of his story.

A BOOK ABOUT YOUR PRAYER

Jabez, you may be surprised that someone has written a whole book just on your little prayer. To be sure, it is a small book, but apparently thousands have read it, and according to the author, "thousands of believers who are applying its truths are seeing miracles happen on a regular basis."

I could not be more pleased. Just as I thrilled to the blessing that God gave to you, so am I happy for each one who today is blessed by your prayer.

I must confess to you, however, that I am a little bit perplexed. At the very beginning of the book I find the words, "ALL RIGHTS RESERVED. No part of this publication may be reproduced, stored in a retrieval system, or transmitted, in any form or by any means—electronic, mechanical, photocopying, recording, or otherwise—without prior written permission." If it is to be a blessing, why can it not be freely shared with all? At the end of the book three pages advertise other books by the same author. I fear that I'm a bit cynical. I think that the author is making a nice penny on your prayer. Forgive me, Jabez. He's not the only one who writes for profit. But what the heck! I reserve no rights on this letter. As far as I'm concerned anyone may reproduce, store in a retrieval system, transmit in any form and by any means, and use it for any legal purpose. What the publisher requires is a different matter. But no reservation comes from me.

Jabez, I thought that you might be interested in the book written about your prayer. I'm going to follow the author's outline and tell you what I think about the book. You may agree more with the author than with me, but I think that he reads more into the prayer than is actually there, makes what I consider to be some unwarranted assumptions, and seems to offer special blessings to all who use your prayer. The assurance of blessings that he promises to all who use your prayer reminds me a great deal of the promises made to those who engage in the Roman Catholic practice of indulgences. Let me know what you think. I would be pleased, but surprised, to hear back from you.

CHAPTER ONE

"JABEZ CALLED ON THE GOD OF ISRAEL"

What can I do for God? Many ask that question and even struggle with it for years. "Sign up to be a gimper for God." That is to be the end of the struggle, and the beginning of a blessed life, says the author of the book about your prayer. A "gimper," we are told, is "someone who always does a little more than what's required or expected."

Jabez, "gimper" is a new word for me; it's not to be found in my language. I've checked the *Oxford Dictionary of the English Language* and it's not to be found. I can only guess the origin of that word.

We play a funny game called football. I won't bore you with the details of the game; it's almost impossible to describe—a ball shaped like a watermelon, and eleven men knocking each other to the ground. About eighty-five years ago, from 1917–1920 there was a great football player at the University of Notre Dame named George Gipp. He died while yet a young man, and on his deathbed he told the Notre Dame football coach, Knute Rockne, that when the Notre Dame football team was in an intense game the coach should rally the team by asking them to "win one for the Gipper." That was meant to do a "little more than was required or expected." I suppose that it means nothing to you but the coach used that challenge in an important game against Army, and Notre Dame won the game.

That's not very important, Jabez, but I think that must be the origin of the word "gimper."

DO SOMETHING FOR GOD

I'm much more concerned about the way the idea of the gimper implies that we are called *to do something for God.*

One of your descendants, far more popular than you, wanted to do something for God. His name was David, one of the most popular names among your descendants. He was King of Israel around 1000 B.C. (Those initials probably mean nothing to you, but we use them to number the years "Before Christ." Certainly you have heard about Christ, though not during your lifetime, yet long before I heard that blessed name).

David wanted to do something for God— build him a house (that is, a temple). God turned the tables on David. Through the prophet Nathan, God spoke to David. "Go and tell my servant David, 'Thus says the LORD: Would you build me a house to dwell in? I have not dwelt in a house since the day I brought up the people of Israel from Egypt to this day . . . Moreover the LORD declares to you that the LORD will make you a house.'" In our Bible that story is recorded in 2 Samuel 7:1-16. Ask Nathan or David to tell you the whole story.

There is a play on words in that narrative. David wanted to build a house (temple) for God, but God didn't want David to "do something" for him. God would be the "doer," the one who would act for David. "I'll make a house (dynasty) for you," said God to David.

Jabez, we find it so tempting to turn the tables on God. Somehow we know that we have violated God, and we want to make things right. But as with David, also with us, God insists that he be the actor. God not only wants to, but *has done* something for us. It all centers in Jesus, who saves us from ourselves and forgives our self-centered-ness. We call what God has done for us "gospel." That word simply means "good news."

We are told to do something for God. We call this "law." We are so prone to confuse law and gospel. The law has such an appeal to us because in our economy we pay for what we get. God's economy is topsy-turvy (that's a strange word that we use to mean "inverted" or "upside down"). In God's economy we who are in deepest need can do absolutely nothing; we can only believe (trust) what God has done for us.

The most amazing thing, Jabez, is that God says that we are saved simply by believing that promise (see Romans 3:28, 6:23 and Mark 16:16). (Jabez, I must ask you to forgive me. I make reference to different parts of our Bible of which you know nothing. However, others who read this letter to you can benefit from those parts of the Bible that I cite.)

He who wrote that little book about your prayer is certain that it will "significantly impact" everyone. He is sure of that because of his own experience and the "testimony of hundreds of others around the world" with whom he has shared "these principles."

PRINCIPLES

Two concerns arise from that certainty. My first concern relates to "these principles." I must admit that there are fellow Believers who understand the Bible to be a set of principles by which people are to live. I do not share that understanding. Principles by which people are to live have to do with "law," or rules. Those who must live by law will understand the Bible as a set of principles. But the Apostle Paul (perhaps you have met him on the other side of the "veil") has some stern words for those who would live by law (principles). "For no human being will be justified in [God's] sight by works of the law, since through the law comes knowledge of sin." Paul continues, "But now the righteousness of God has been manifested apart from law, although the law and the prophets bear witness to it . . ." (Romans 3:20-21). Paul even goes so far to say that "Christ is the end of the law . . ." (Romans 10:4).

Jabez, I understand our Bible quite differently than as a set of principles by which to live. If I must characterize the whole Bible I understand it more as a love letter in which God tells me what he has done for me, because I am unable to do anything for myself, or for God. Before God I am in deepest need, and can only thank, praise, serve, love, and obey him.

A MODEL PRAYER

My second concern, Jabez, arises from the idea that your prayer should be the model prayer for everyone. I find no warrant for that contention. If it has been helpful to some I thank God for that. However, there are other prayers in the Bible. Each may or may not be useful to any particular individual, and not all who prayed in the Bible received what they wanted. Jonah prayed, if not in word, at least by his action (see Jonah 1:1-3, 3:3), and was not relieved of his responsibility. Paul prayed to be relieved from some physical ailment, and it was not granted (2 Corinthians 12:7-9). Jesus prayed to be spared death, but was not spared (Matthew 26:39). Any and all of those prayers can be useful to a Believer, as can yours, Jabez. I only object that yours should be singled out as the great prayer for all in order to receive a super blessing. If there is a single prayer for every Believer, perhaps it is the prayer that Jesus taught his disciples. We call it the Lord's Prayer (Matthew 6:9-13). Even that need not be simply recited, but rather seen as a pattern for prayer.

GOD WANTS TO GIVE

In the book about your prayer, we are told that "your Father longs to give you so much more than you have ever thought to ask for." I fear that may be true Jabez, but it has the ring of the pursuit of this world—fame, wealth, power, and success. If God chooses to give that to some, may they use it all as a blessing to serve others. But it may very well be that God chooses to give us a cross to bear, just as he gave one to Jesus. That cross may be a child with cerebral palsy, muscular dystrophy, or multiple sclerosis. It may be an aged parent for whom to give care. It may be a job in a nursing home that pays poorly but requires great compassion and service. Yes, indeed, God may want to give much more than one ever thought or asked for, and in the bearing of that cross many find their blessing.

The cross is much more a symbol of Christian suffering and faithfulness than the more dangerous "blessings" of fame, fortune, power, and success.

I am not particularly concerned about what God chooses to give to others. I am deeply concerned about a promise, or at least a very powerful suggestion, that encourages a "give me" posture. That posture stands in opposition to the example of Jesus, who always stood in a posture of giving.

We know so little about you, Jabez. I think it quite unfair to make a judgment about you, any judgment, based on a one-sentence prayer that has been preserved for us.

Is it really true that "things ended extraordinarily well" for you, as the writer of the book about your prayer claims? That's quite an assumption. Again, we know too little about you to make that assertion. We know only that God granted what you requested, and that you were more noble than your brothers. We know absolutely nothing about your brothers; consequently, we can't even make a guess as to how honorable you were.

EMBARRASSINGLY SUSPICIOUS

It's time to draw this little section to a close, but the book that makes so much of your prayer says that the "unclaimed blessings" that God has waiting for us seem an impossibility—"even embarrassingly suspicious in our self-serving day." It sure does! That confession belongs in capital letters. Not your prayer, Jabez, but the extravagant claims made on the basis of your prayer, sound exceedingly self-serving, and quite contrary to the way of the cross that Jesus walked. It is embarrassingly self-serving in the light of Jesus' statement to his disciples, "If any man would come after me, let him deny himself and take up his cross and follow me. For whoever would save his life will lose it, and whoever loses his life for my sake will find it" (Matthew 16:24-25).

CHAPTER TWO

"OH, THAT YOU WOULD BLESS ME INDEED!"

I found a most wonderful statement in this chapter. It was like finding a beautiful rose in a field of weeds. It is beautiful in its own right; I'll include it for you.

A ROSE AMONG WEEDS

"Notice a radical aspect of Jabez's prayer for blessing: *He left it entirely up to God to decide what the blessings would be and where, when, and how Jabez would receive them.*" This kind of radical trust in God's good intentions toward us has nothing in common with the popular gospel that you should ask God for a Cadillac, a six-figure income, or some other material sign that you have found a way to cash in on your connection with him.

That statement about leaving it in God's hands rang a bell with me, Jabez. I wanted to jump up and say, "Yes, he's got it right! Hurrah!" I applaud that understanding of God's blessings and never want to let it go.

SELF-CENTERED PRAYER

I don't want to diminish that statement in the least, but two things strike me. How can anyone know what your hopes were when you offered that prayer? We may hope that you were open to whatever blessing God chose to give to you. On the other hand, if you are like the majority of humankind (and why should I expect otherwise?), you may have been very self-centered in your hope and prayer. Indeed, in granting your prayer for a blessing God may have given you something quite different than that for which you hoped or expected. It is an unwarranted reading into the Bible to say that you left it entirely up to God to decide what your blessing should be. In fact, you say quite clearly that you want more territory. There is only a limited amount of real estate. If you get more, someone else must get less.

My second concern is that while the statement resonates most positively with me I find it quite out of character with the rest of the book. So much of the book seems to be centered in the self. Even when asking God for a blessing, the central concern is *my* blessing, something that *I* get.

SPEAKING AND HEARING

I must add a note at this point, Jabez. Communication is very difficult. That is especially true with written communication. There is no body language to accompany the words, no gestures, no voice inflection, no facial expression. There can be quite a difference between what the writer intends and what the reader "hears." Further, in written communication there is no opportunity to ask for clarification. Consequently, I readily admit that I am responding to what I "hear" in that book that was written about your prayer. If the author had something in mind other than what I "heard," then the problem is either with his inability to state his case clearly, or my inability to "hear" correctly.

That was a bit of a digression, but I thought it important to note.

There are several issues in this chapter to which I must respond.

A FULLER LIFE

There is a mention of wanting to "experience a fuller Christian life." The nature of that "fuller life" is not made clear. It is only said that "some men and women of faith rise above the rest . . . they think and pray differently than those around them."

That kind of language makes me very nervous, Jabez. It sounds much like a return to the monastic mentality of the Middle Ages. (I know that I'm using terms totally unfamiliar to you. We refer to the years from about 600 A.D. to about 1400 A.D. as the Middle Ages. They conclude just before the time that the reformation of the church began in the sixteenth century. Perhaps you have met Martin Luther and John Calvin. They can clarify words like "Middle Ages," and "reformation of the church" for you.)

Monasticism promised a "fuller and higher" state of Christian living. It amounted to a withdrawal from life in the world to a life of prayer and meditation. Some branches of monasticism also included a good deal of service to others. That is both noteworthy and commendable. What is not commendable is the idea that a certain class of Christians possesses a "higher" or "fuller" Christian life.

A very convincing argument can be made that the reformation of the church was a protest against the monastic quest for, and promise of, a higher and fuller Christian life.

Our old sinful nature, Jabez, hasn't changed since your day. There is that natural urge to stand a little bit higher than others, a little closer to God, on the basis of what we do.

I'm sad to tell you that there is still an element within our Protestant tradition (again, you'll have to ask Luther to explain "Protestant") that is more closely tied to Roman Catholicism prior to the Reformation than it is to the Protestant reaction against that monastic idea of a higher or fuller Christian life.

BLESSING

Now I want to get to the heart of this cry for a blessing. Is it really true that the biblical sense of the verb "to bless" means "to ask for or to impart supernatural favor"? That is what the author of the book about you says, Jabez. Let's think about that.

I don't want to be too simplistic. I know that the word "blessing" is used in the Bible in several different contexts. But the most succinct statement on that word comes from Jesus in what is called his Sermon on the Mount. I'd like to share that with you because it was not available to you in your day, although you may have heard about it in later years.

"Blessed are the poor in spirit,

   for theirs is the kingdom of heaven.

"Blessed are those who mourn,

   for they shall be comforted.

"Blessed are the meek,

   for they shall inherit the earth.

"Blessed are those who hunger and thirst

   for righteousness,

   for they shall be satisfied.

"Blessed are the merciful,

   for they shall obtain mercy.

"Blessed are the pure in heart,

> for they shall see God.
> "Blessed are the peacemakers,
>> for they shall be called sons of God.
> "Blessed are those who are persecuted
>> for righteousness' sake,
>> for theirs is the kingdom of heaven.
> "Blessed are you when men revile you
>> and persecute you and utter all kinds
>> of evil against you falsely
>> on my account" (Matthew 5:3-11).

Were those the kinds of things that you had in mind when you cried to God to be blessed? We will never know. Perhaps you've even forgotten. But these are the qualities of which I was thinking when I said that it may not only be true that God wants to give us more than we ever thought to ask for, but I *fear* that it may be true. I suspect that not one in a hundred, probably not one in a thousand, has those qualities in mind when asking God for a blessing; and I certainly didn't sense that cry in the book written about your prayer. On the contrary, I sense that in asking God for a blessing I should expect something quite palatable to my natural self-centered tendencies; if not a Cadillac or six-figure income, at least some "success" that I can place in my religious trophy case.

SUPERNATURAL?

The certainty that blessings are identified as "supernatural favors" also causes me pain. That again is a reversion to medieval Roman Catholic thought in which the natural was almost ripped from the hand of God so that the church could sell the supernatural. Again, it was the reformation of the church in the sixteenth century under the leadership of Martin Luther that reclaimed the natural as belonging to God.

Jabez, I do not want to suggest for a moment that our God does not employ the supernatural at times, but I am so pleased that the great majority of God's blessings comes through that which is natural. The greatest blessing of my life is a dear loving wife. In retrospect, because we are both people of faith, we see the hand of God uniting a boy from a small rural community in North Dakota with a girl from urban Washington. We affirm God's guiding hand in that union, but we see nothing supernatural about it. Three wonderful children, two great sons-in-law, a beloved daughter-in-law, and five precious grandchildren are among the richest of God's blessings in our lives. Nothing could be more natural than love, marriage, children, and grandchildren.

A further listing of blessings would be exhaustive and exhausting. I have said enough so that you can recount your own blessings, and recognize that the great majority of them come to you quite naturally from God's providential and benevolent hand.

Yes, Jabez, I have received supernatural blessings too. How God could make me his child in baptism when I was too young to even know what was happening, and feed me with the very body and blood of Jesus Christ in Holy Communion are supernatural acts beyond my comprehension. For those blessings, and for the blessing of life in community with other Believers, I bow in reverential and eternal thanks. (As for baptism and Holy Communion, you better ask Jesus to explain. I doubt that either Martin Luther or John Calvin understand those supernatural mysteries better than I.)

I think of two other supernatural blessings. The simple fact that I or anyone else believes the gospel is a miracle. That I should be accounted righteous because of what Jesus did for me two thousand years ago is not a natural rational deduction. Only the power of God can accomplish the miracle of faith.

Jesus said to his disciples, "If any man would come after me, let him deny himself and take up his cross and follow me" (Mark 8:34). I am sure that you will agree that it is not natural to deny oneself. Self-denial for the sake of Jesus Christ and the gospel is a supernatural event accomplished only by a miracle of God.

Those supernatural events of new life with God through baptism, Christ's presence in the Lord's Supper, the gift of faith, and the ability to deny oneself are miracles far greater than any serendipitous event encountered in day-to-day living.

I only care that we not place so much attention on seeking supernatural blessings that we miss God's blessings that come to us through natural means, for God is as much Lord over the natural as the supernatural.

MIRACLES

"Your life will become marked by miracles," claims the man who wrote the book about your prayer. That's the "guaranteed by-product of sincerely seeking His blessing."

This is just another, perhaps religious, way to remove God from the natural world and confine him to a sphere from which he can interact with humanity primarily, if not exclusively, through an interruption of the natural. Such understanding of God's activity has some similarities to the rationalistic deism of the seventeenth and eighteenth centuries wherein God was divorced from his creation, presumably to take a vacation until the course of history, running on natural law, may reach its end.

The difference between rationalistic deism and life lived from one miracle to another is that the latter does not understand God to be on a long vacation. Rather, God regularly interrupts the natural course of history and individual lives to interject an unexpected element. God is, nevertheless, in both cases, quite removed from natural life.

INTERPRETATION

Oh, Jabez, how dangerous the Bible is. The great message, precious beyond any human words, is so misused to support a great variety of private opinions, ideas, programs, and ventures. I grieve when a sentence is pulled out of its context to support an individual prejudice or argument. I am particularly grieved when that trick is used by one who is supposed to be particularly trained in the interpretation of the Bible.

We must ask, we are told, in order to receive God's blessings. Then St. James is quoted to support the contention. "You do not have, because you do not ask," said James (James 4:2). No mention is made of the very next sentence, which continues the thought, "You ask and do not receive because you ask wrongly, to spend it on your passions" (James 4:3).

St. Matthew 7:7 is quoted, "Ask, and it will be given you." As I noted earlier in this letter, Jabez, St. Paul asked to be relieved of a bodily ailment and did not receive what he requested (2 Corinthians 12:7-9).

I have no doubt that God is the great Giver. As a good and benevolent Father gives to his children everything that he thinks to be good for them, so our heavenly Father is lavish in giving us what is needful and useful. But to dangle a couple of sentences from the Bible as a basis to catch the unreflective person, and make promises that aren't substantiated from the record of the whole Bible, is a great misuse of the Bible. And to suggest that God's blessing are withheld because they are not requested from God flies directly in the face of the words of Jesus, who said that God's blessings come to all people regardless of their righteousness. Jesus said of God, ". . . he makes his sun rise on the evil and on the good, and sends rain on the just and on the unjust" (Matthew 5:45).

Martin Luther had it right when explaining the meaning to the phrase in the Lord's Prayer, "Give us this day our daily bread." Luther said,

"God gives daily bread even *without our prayer,* to all people, though sinful, but we ask in this prayer that he will help us to realize this and to receive our daily bread with thanks."

Doesn't that sound more in tune with what Jesus said, Jabez?

ASKING FOR IT

One last comment on this chapter. "What counts is knowing who you want to be and asking for it." Am I to set the course of my life? It sure sounds like it from that statement. I decide, then I ask God to support my decision? Preposterous!

Three prime examples from the Bible come to mind that throw that idea into the garbage can of rancid baloney. You know Moses, I presume. Has he told you how he resisted God's call? I know that you don't have a Bible, but Moses can tell you about it. I can read about it in chapters three and four of Exodus.

Jeremiah didn't want to be a prophet. Ask him. I note it in Jeremiah 1:6. Ask Jeremiah about the poem he wrote decrying that he was born because his lot had been to be a prophet (Jeremiah 20:7-18).

Ask Paul whether he wanted to be a disciple of Jesus Christ. He sure didn't ask for it. We who have a Bible can find a record of the violent way in which he was "defeated" into serving Jesus (Acts 26:9-23).

To seek God's direction in every area of life is most commendable, indeed desirable, but to say, "Know what you want to be and ask for it" sounds too much like the dramatic but self-centered line, "I am the master of my fate: / I am the captain of my soul." I know what I want to be, the goals that I have set for myself, the course that my life should take; now God please get behind me and make my dream come true. That is certainly not the note of Jesus when on the night before his death he submitted to God's intention and cried, "not as I will, but as thou wilt" (Matthew 26:39).

Jabez, do you see how this whole program is so self-centered? I hope that you do.

CHAPTER THREE

"OH, THAT YOU WOULD ENLARGE MY TERRITORY"

Like many prayers in my day, yours also was quite self-centered. You simply wanted more real estate.

EISEGESIS AND EXEGESIS

We are told, however, that there was more to your prayer than a request for more land. We are told that the prayer's context and its success indicate that you wanted not just real estate, but "more influence, more responsibility, and more opportunity *to make a mark for the God of Israel.*"

Another bit of rancid baloney is there peddled for the gullible. There is almost no context at all that may help us understand the motive for your prayer. The only comment made about you is that you were more honorable than your brothers. As I noted earlier, we know nothing at all about your brothers, so the comment about you may be like saying that ice is warmer than liquid hydrogen.

The result of your prayer is no greater help in determining the motive for your prayer. That "God granted what he asked" says absolutely nothing about your motive.

It is clear to me, Jabez that you were a sinner like the rest of us—self-centered, always seeking more for yourself. By that recognition I certainly don't mean to paint you as a reprobate to be scorned. I simply mean to recognize you as one of the rest of us. Frankly, I am heartened to find one like you in the pages of the Bible. Indeed I find many like you in those pages. It gives me more confidence that our Bible presents people as they really are, and does not give them a religious whitewash job.

The fact that God granted you what you requested says a lot more about God than it does about you. Our God is gracious and answers the prayers of sinners. If God is going to answer any prayer he *must* answer the prayer of sinners: there are no others to offer prayer to him (see Romans 3:9-10, 23).

(I hope that you understand what I mean when I say that only sinners pray to God. By now you have undoubtedly heard the ceaseless prayer of praise by the sinless holy angels, and the prayers of the saints who now rest from their labors, you among them. Those prayers of praise, however, take me well beyond the point of your prayer, and the book written about it.)

Neither the context nor the result give any hint as to what motivated your request for more territory. I take your prayer at face value. You simply wanted more for yourself. But, Jabez, I am dismayed and exasperated, not at your prayer, but the confident statement that your prayer was motivated by a desire to "make a mark for the God of Israel." There is not the slightest shred of evidence to support that claim. It is no more than an attempt to put a pious spin on a self-centered prayer.

We have a technical term for the kind of biblical interpretation that reads things into the Bible that are not there. We call it *eisegesis*. Eisegesis expresses the interpreter's own ideas and bias rather than the true meaning of the text. Real biblical interpretation begins with *exegesis,* which means to take something out from the text. To engage in eisegesis is kind of like being so intent upon finding diamonds in a gravel pit that the searcher places a diamond ring in the gravel pit then retrieved as proof that diamonds are indeed to be found there. That is a most despicable way to interpret the word of God. One can make the Bible say anything one chooses with that kind of interpretation. Perhaps you understand why I refer to such pious pranks as "rancid baloney."

A SECULAR PRAYER

The clearest indication that your prayer is being interpreted according to the ways of this world, and not according to the mind of Christ, is the statement, "If Jabez had worked on Wall Street, he might have prayed, 'Lord, increase the value of my investment portfolios.'" Indeed that may have been your prayer, and God may have granted your request. But it is no less a prayer grounded in the ways of this world. I am not so astonished at the prayer, for thousands of self-centered prayers just like it storm the throne of God. I am astonished that a pastor of the church of Jesus Christ affirms and even encourages such a prayer.

The encouragement of such a prayer has nothing to do with the mind of Christ. The Apostle Paul encourages a totally different orientation. "Have this mind among yourselves, which is yours in Christ Jesus, who, though he was in the form of God, did not count equality with God a thing to be grasped, but emptied himself, taking the form of a servant, being born in the likeness of men. And being found in human form he humbled himself and became obedient unto death, even death on a cross" (Philippians 2:5-8). "Lord, increase the value of my investment portfolio." The two go together like sawdust on an ice cream sundae!

I don't mean to embarrass you, Jabez. My prayers, I am sure, are no better than yours. I am just blessed that mine have not been put in print for people to read over the centuries. If you are embarrassed, take heart; your prayer is, like most, prayed to a God of boundless love. It is not your prayer but the book written about your prayer that gives me spiritual and intellectual indigestion.

GLAMOUR AND MOTIVATION

I found a second rose in a field of weeds, Jabez. There is the suggestion that the highest form your prayer might take may sound something like this:

"O God and King, please expand my opportunities and my impact in such a way that I touch more lives for Your glory." At least that prayer is in the spirit of Jesus, who charged his followers to make disciples by baptism followed by teaching.

But alas, the weeds only get deeper and more ugly. We are told that our author challenged a college student body to "ask God for Trinidad." (Trinidad is a small island in the ocean a long way from where you lived.) One summer 126 students and faculty went to Trinidad to minister through teaching, building, song, drama, and so on. That was nice, even commendable. But two things strike me, Jabez.

As far as I can tell the island wasn't won for God by that visitation. Hopefully, a few lives were positively touched. The final result of that visit, or any endeavor in the name of Jesus Christ, can never be known. Only at the close of history will the effect of that visit to Trinidad be known. I just don't get the big deal about going to Trinidad from

Sacramento, California. It may be more glamorous and exciting than remaining in Sacramento and teaching children there the love of God, helping the homeless find shelter, and the unemployed find work, but I certainly don't see it as a greater service to humanity in the name of God.

The second concern is the ability of some people to motivate others to action. I wonder if you had that kind in your day. We do today. They are masters of persuasion. However, just because they can motivate others to do extraordinary things, or perform ordinary things extraordinarily well, is no certainty that they represent God. Motivational speakers are usually charismatic personalities adept at motivating others to sell various products, go door-to-door seeking support for political candidates, or, in the extreme, to go to Guyana to commit mass suicide.

I learned nothing about your prayer or about God's will for my life from the story of that summer trip to Trinidad.

NATURAL OR SUPERNATURAL

The man who wrote about your prayer tells of two cases in which, by praying for "greater territory," he was able to help a young couple save their marriage and free a woman from worry that she might not recognize the anti-Christ. I am pleased to hear of anyone who is helped in any way. But those two stories were preceded by the statement, "As your opportunities expand, your ability and resources supernaturally increase, too."

Again, God is removed from the natural so that all good can be called "supernatural." Such antics may elevate the level of excitement in deeds done, but it hardly does God any honor. The two incidents recited came along quite naturally. One need only keep eyes and ears open to service opportunities.

A PERSONAL EXPERIENCE

As I write this I am on a cruise ship. (Excuse me, Jabez. You surely have no idea what a cruise ship is. It's a ship on which mostly rich people or people who have saved a lot of money embark from a port, eat for about a week, and come back to the place from which they started. It's a bit more than that, but that is a fairly accurate description of a cruise.)

On this cruise I did a little investigating. I did not pray your prayer in advance. I did not ask God for any opportunity to serve him. I just kept my eyes and ears open, and I sensed a need. It was nothing glamorous like claiming an island for God. I'll share it with you.

Two room stewards on two different cruise lines have confirmed approximately the same story. They work eleven hours a day, seven days a week, with a few additional hours on the day of embarkation. For those hours of service their guaranteed salary is fifty dollars per month, plus food that is left over from the passenger's menu! (This reminds me of the story of the rich man and Lazarus, as recorded in Luke 16:1-31. Perhaps you have met Lazarus. I expect that you have not met the rich man.) Any additional income must come from gratuities. Their guaranteed income is something less than fifteen cents per hour. It seems that usually young people from developing countries are exploited in this way. I could describe the condition further, but that is not the point of this letter. I find that condition to be more obscene than any picture ever published by *Playboy Magazine.* (There is no use trying to describe that magazine to you.)

Jabez, I mention these circumstances to you only to say that I have composed a letter that I will send to a friend in the United States Congress. (Members of Congress make the laws by which we must live in our country.) I have asked him to investigate this condition and require all cruise ships that dock in a United States port to pay a minimum wage to all employees. I am confident that he will act. If he does not I will seek relief from other quarters that may shame Congress into action.

What's the point of this story? Only that I did not pray your prayer. It was simply a conscience, at least moderately informed by the Word of God and the life of Jesus, that saw a human need and a way to try to relieve it. Service in the name of God most often happens in the least glamorous ways. I don't expect that when I disembark the ship any state room steward will rush to the deck rail and shout a word of thanks to me.

I must conclude my comments on this chapter by saying that rather than asking for more territory, I find plenty to do in the territory that God has given to me without my asking. My prayer is not for more territory, but for greater faithfulness in the territory that has already been given to me.

Jesus once told a story about three stewards whose master gave them five, three, and one talent. Each was to give an account to the master as to how they had cared for the talents. Those who had been faithful were later given more without their asking. The issue was not more territory, but faithfulness in the territory already assigned.

CHAPTER FOUR

"OH, THAT YOUR HAND WOULD BE WITH ME"

This is a good chapter, Jabez. I have prayed similar words many times. You and I and all mortals are inadequate to speak the truth without the presence of God guiding us. Jesus told his disciples, (I trust that you have met them by now. You've had more than two thousand years to get acquainted.) "When the Spirit of truth comes, he will guide you into all the truth" (John 16:13).

DEPENDENCE
A strong emphasis on "dependence" characterizes the first half of this chapter.

Finally I can make reference to someone who preceded you. You recall the story of Adam and Eve in the Garden of Eden. In that story I read, "Then the LORD God said, 'It is not good that the man should be alone; I'll make him a helper fit for him'" (Genesis 2:18). I understand that to be a strong statement that we humans are created to be dependent on one another. Independence, autonomy, going it alone are transparent clues to our sinful nature. Indeed Jabez, I agree; we are created to be dependent on God and on one another. Of course, in the search for truth we may be aided by others, but we are most dependent on God since others are afflicted with the same malady as we—sin.

The emphasis on dependence is marvelous, admirable, and in complete harmony with the message of the entire Bible. However, the emphasis is on dependence not so that the dependent can be successful. New business opportunities are mentioned along with ministry opportunities.

SUCCESS

Jabez, I'm not sure whether your language had an equivalent to our word "success." I rather hope that it did not, for "success" is a very slippery word. In our culture success is usually measured by wealth, fame, or power. Frequently they are merged. Those with the most wealth, fame, or power are considered to be successful. That's not what I hear in the pages of the Bible, and it is not what I see in the life of Jesus. Success, if such a concept is even applicable to a Christian Believer, seems to be in terms of faithfulness.

The Bible talks about the "blessed" person, but never the "successful" person.

Those who have been faithful, noted in the pages of the Bible and the annals of history, most often have not been people of wealth, fame, or power. Peter and Paul were "successful" because they were faithful. It cost them their lives. Other faithful followers throughout the centuries, including the century in which I live, have paid that same supreme sacrifice as Peter and Paul.

Dependence? Yes! For the sake of success? No! Dependence only for the fortitude to remain faithful.

PURE BALONEY

I said earlier in this letter that he who wrote about your prayer read more into it than is warranted. I will give you a concrete illustration of that fact. The author points out that you did not begin your prayer by asking that God's hand be with you. You asked that later in the prayer, he asserts, because you didn't know earlier that you needed God's hand: "But when his boundaries got moved out, and the kingdom-sized tasks of God's agenda started coming at him, Jabez knew that he needed a divine hand—and fast."

That statement sounds as though you prayed that single sentence prayer over a period of several months. I timed it, and it took me about four seconds from the beginning of the prayer to the phrase, "and that your hand would be with me." Are we to believe that at the beginning of your prayer you didn't sense a need for God's hand to be with you, but within the space of four seconds your territory had been enlarged to the extent that you were overwhelmed and recognized your dependent need? That's preposterous! It's the kind of thinking that contributes to the belief of some nonbelievers that Christians speak nonsense.

Nevertheless, in spite of some preposterous claims and dangerous inferences about success, this is still the best chapter in the book to this point. I resonate most positively when I read, "That's why you could call God's hand on you 'the touch of greatness.' You do not become great; you become dependent on the strong hand of God." Later in the chapter some wonderful things are said about "the hand of the Lord," as that phrase is found in the Bible.

Jabez, I wish that the chapter had ended on such a high note. It does not.

MORE SUCCESS STORIES

Another success story is offered. The details don't matter because you know nothing of Long Island or magic shows, and I expect that you were not much for "strategy."

I'm not much taken with success stories. Those stories provide a wonderful motivational technique to inspire others to great efforts. Athletic coaches can use them to great advantage. "Win one for the Gipper!" In all avenues of human endeavor, success stories are useful for motivation. I'm just not impressed with such stories in the context of our common faith, Jabez. I'll tell you why. Thousands of Believers have prayed ardently on bended knee for success on their mission or ministry and have not been rewarded in any observable way. Have they not prayed with sufficient earnest and passion? It is the character of our faith that we believe even when we do not see observable results or "success."

For example, Adoniram Judson was a pioneer missionary to Burma—present day Myanmar. (Burma is a country thousands of miles from where you lived, and thousands of miles from where I live). Judson's son said that his father labored thirteen years before he realized his first convert to the Christian faith. Then he added, "If you sacrifice without success, someone will succeed after you. If you succeed without sacrifice, someone has sacrificed before you."

The whole emphasis on success just doesn't square with the call to faithful service. Believers don't keep score; they are content merely to serve.

I don't want to be misunderstood, Jabez. I am delighted whenever I hear of one or a thousand who have found freedom, forgiveness, hope, and purpose in life under the lordship of Jesus Christ. I thank God for each story of one who has been captured by the Master. I just don't like the emphasis on success that is so much a part of this world's mentality, and so foreign to discipleship under Jesus Christ.

IT'S UP TO ME?

I would prefer not to conclude on a negative note because I really do appreciate the strong positive emphasis on dependence upon God. But I would not be complete in my description to you, Jabez if I did not note what belongs more to the Enlightenment (that's another strange term that is part of the disinformation of this world) of France in the eighteenth century than to any Believer in your day or mine. It's the little phrase, "It's up to you."

It certainly wasn't "up to" the Apostle Paul or Martin Luther. The hand of God grabbed them in spite of themselves and used them for his own purposes. The twelve disciples didn't "decide for

Jesus," they were called by Jesus. Many months after they began to follow him Jesus had to remind them, "You did not choose me, but I chose you" (John 15:16).

Jabez, I think that you know that it was not "up to you." We are only told that God honored your prayer. God certainly was not obligated to honor it.

So with that note I conclude my comments on what was essentially a positive chapter, which emphasized the need to depend upon God.

CHAPTER FIVE

"OH, THAT YOU WOULD KEEP ME FROM EVIL"

This chapter is even better than the last.

The call to flee from evil is not so much a brilliant insight as it is a recognition of the awesome and terrible power of evil. You might expect that rational people would recognize that destructive power and naturally flee from it. That is certainly not true in my day; I expect that it was not true in your day either. Apparently only those who pay attention to God's warning recognize evil for the threat it really is.

FREEDOM FROM MYSELF

Perhaps we fail to recognize evil because we all participate in it so naturally.

When the people with whom I worship God gather for that purpose we occasionally begin our worship with these words. "Almighty God, we confess to you that we are by nature sinful and unclean." I mention that confession of sin because it confirms our natural participation in evil. (I think that I need not persuade you that sin is evil.) Because we are so intrinsically tied to evil, we do not naturally recognize it.

Let me try to illustrate with the following, Jabez. White is not easily seen against a white background; black is not recognized against a black background. The same can be said for any color.

God must call our attention to evil and its destructive power. Only by believing God do we flee from it. In fleeing from evil we are actually fleeing from ourselves. That comes with the greatest difficulty and is accomplished only when God's Spirit breaks through to set us free.

I found this chapter particularly useful because it warns about the dangers of success. Of course, the success against which we are warned is success as measured by this world. That success is suspect from the beginning. But granted the definition, the warning is more than warranted.

DEBUNKING SUCCESS

But before I say more, Jabez, I think that the best way to combat the idea of success is to forswear, abjure, and deny the definition. I certainly don't mean to live in fantasy land, nor deny that wealth is wealth, fame is fame, and power is power. I deny that the achievement of any or all of those three constitutes success. If any of the three should befall an individual, let it be; but do not pretend that such constitutes success.

In my day I hear people talk about being blessed financially. I often wonder if the correct verb is used. May we not with equal validity say that we have been threatened with financial gain?

It seems to me, Jabez, that if the idea of success is removed from any of those three issues, we need to speak of them neither as blessings nor threats. They are, we might say, value-neutral.

I guess that I got a bit carried away on that issue. I mention it because the tenor of the whole book about your prayer seems to promote the idea of success, and then warns against its danger. I thoroughly oppose the presentation of a life with God as a ticket to success if we only pray your prayer; I heartily agree with the warning of its dangers.

THE NATURE OF EVIL

In the flight from evil we are told of a plane trip in which the two sitting on the right and on the left of the author each opened a pornographic magazine. The author prayed to be delivered from such evil. The two on either side both swore out loud and put away their magazines.

Whatever you may think about that story, I only wish that I could be so easily delivered from evil. I do not mean to diminish the serious issue of pornography. I expect that some form of pornography was available is your day, too, although I doubt that it was so pervasive and available as it is in my day.

Pornography is a serious moral blight on our society. It robs women and men, but especially women, of their humanity, and treats them as objects to be used for personal enjoyment. In addition, pornography appeals to the basest of human instincts. By appealing to such base desires it inhibits the higher and more noble capacities that God has given to us. I have nothing good to say on behalf of pornography.

But Jabez, I trust that you too know that the evil of pornography can be dismissed simply by closing one's eyes. The evil from which I pray to be delivered comes much less from external stimuli than it does from deep within me. I cannot so easily escape that. So, when I pray, "Oh, that you would keep me from evil," or "deliver us from evil" as our Lord taught us to pray, since I am more likely to pattern my prayer as Jesus suggested, I am really praying that God would deliver me from myself. Perhaps it would be more accurate to say that my deepest prayer is that God would protect me from myself and from my natural selfish wants and desires.

I wonder what you think, Jabez. I read this statement in the book about your prayer: "Without a temptation, we would not sin." I think that is probably true, but this is not much different from saying, "If we were unconscious, under anesthesia, or sleeping we would not sin."

Simply being alive and conscious places us all under temptation—temptation to satisfy our natural self-centered urges. All that is self-centered is sin, indeed the primordial sin. That which is self-centered cannot be God-centered.

We are told correctly that "being tempted is not the same thing as sinning." The great Reformer of the Church, Martin Luther, once said about temptation, "You cannot keep the birds from flying over your head; but you can keep them from making a nest in your hair."

Nevertheless, no one is completely successful in the fight against temptation. St. Paul said, "None is righteous, no, not one" (Romans 3:10); and "all have sinned and fall short of the glory of God" (Romans 3:23). Consequently, all who live with God live not on the basis of successfully fleeing temptation but only on the basis of the forgiveness of sin.

NO JESUS AND NO FORGIVENESS

I am more than a bit dismayed, Jabez, that in the book there is no mention of the forgiveness of sin;

the whole emphasis is on what I must do in following your prayer. Neither do I read anything about the victory that Jesus Christ has won for me by his death and resurrection. There is nothing about my baptism into the death and resurrection of Jesus. (Ask Paul to tell you what he wrote to the Christians in Rome. In our Bibles I find his clear statement in Romans 6:4). I have no doubt that even though you lived about 1,500 years before Jesus was born you know all about him now, for he is your savior as well as mine.

One of the best statements in the entire book is the following: "Do we really understand how far the American Dream is from God's dream for us? We're steeped in a culture that worships freedom, independence, personal rights, and the pursuit of pleasure. We respect people who sacrifice to get what they want. But to be a living sacrifice? To be crucified to the self?"

I'm afraid that if I comment on that statement I'll spoil it. I'll let it stand as it is.

The chapter issues an urgent call to prayer without which any Believer will lose in the battle with temptation and evil. I heartily concur. However, because you are apparently the proto-typical pray-er I need not tell *you* any more on that subject!

CHAPTER SIX

"JABEZ WAS MORE HONORABLE THAN HIS BROTHERS."

So it says, and so you were. Unfortunately we are told nothing about your brothers, nor are we told by the author of First Chronicles why you were considered to be more honorable than they. The one who wrote that book about your prayer thinks that he knows the answer to that question: He asserts that your prayer earned you a "'more honorable' award from God." Hmmm . . .

EARNING AWARDS

Two things must be said about that statement. First, it is another case of reading into the Bible what one wants it to say. Although the Bible *does* say that you were more honorable than your brothers, it certainly *does not* say that you were more honorable because of your prayer.

Second, you and I both know that we never "earn" any award from God. To speak of "earning" something from God sounds like pre-Vatican II Roman Catholic talk. (Oh, Jabez, I apologize again. You probably have not heard of Vatican II— or, more formally, the Second Vatican Council. It's a bit of church bureaucracy, important to the church today, but mere trivia in your realm. Vatican II was the second time that the Roman Catholic bishops gathered in Vatican City—a place surrounded by Rome. It took place between 1962 and 1965, and one of its primary purposes was to bring that part of the Christian church into the modern era. Many good things happened at that council). Prior to Vatican II, Roman Catholics were encouraged to "earn" merits with God. Today that note has been considerably softened in the Roman Catholic Church. When the author, a Protestant pastor, writing about your prayer speaks of "earning" any award from God, he reveals himself to be a throwback to old Roman Catholic ideas against which the Protestant reformers fought. It indicates that the old self-centered sinful nature has won a battle and the Reformation has lost a bit of ground.

So Jabez, we simply do not know why you were more honorable than your brothers. Perhaps you don't either. In fact, you may never have known it for the account was written long after your day, and we are not told that you thought of yourself as more honorable.

The author wonders about the other people named in the genealogy in which your prayer is quoted. What happened to them? How did God reward them, if they were rewarded at all? The writer of the book of Chronicles does not tell us about the others, but the book about your prayer implies that they got nothing because they asked for nothing. Again, another unwarranted assumption, another reading into the Bible something that is not there.

Jabez, there are thousands upon thousands whose lives have been blessed beyond measure simply because of the gracious loving kindness of God. I am included in that great company of the abundantly blessed, and it is not because of what I did or what I prayed. It is simply because of the grace of a benevolent Father who lavishes his blessing on his unworthy children. Therefore, as an old Christian once said, "I surely ought to thank, pray, serve, love, and obey him."

No, Jabez, neither you nor I "earned" any "award" from God. We are recipients of grace alone! (Did Paul tell you what he wrote to the Christians in Ephesus? "For by grace you have been saved through faith; and this is not your own doing, it is the gift of God—not because of works, lest any man should boast." I find that in my Bible in Ephesians 2:8-9).

MORE BALONEY

"To say that you want to be 'more honorable' in God's eyes is not arrogance or self-centeredness." Baloney! Although we are told, "'More honorable' describes what God thinks; it is not credit we take for ourselves," the two little words, "I want" or "you want," betray the self-centeredness of the desire. On the contrary, "Humble yourselves therefore under the mighty hand of God, that in due time he may exalt you," says Peter (1 Peter 5:6). According to St. Matthew, Jesus also said, "whoever exalts himself will be humbled, and whoever humbles himself will be exalted" (Matthew 23:12).

No Jabez, both you and I know that we are not to seek honor with God. That desire for

honor—with God or with anybody else—
comes all too easily. We need not seek it. We
need only seek humility and service if our lives
are to be patterned after Jesus. That comes with
great effort.

It's not just an unfortunate use of words,
Jabez. A page later we read, "I've noticed that
winning honor nearly always means leaving
mediocre expectations and comfortable assumptions behind." "Winning honor!" There can be no
mistake. Again, an active verb indicates that it is
something that you and I and every reader must
do. That's not only baloney; it's rancid baloney.
Martin Luther lived in vain, and Jesus died in vain,
if that "merit badge" baloney is peddled in the
name of Christianity.

SUPERSAINTS

The book about your prayer goes on to mention
"supersaints." Even though we are told that there

are ". . . very few supersaints listed among those God has placed on his honor roll," (Hebrews 11) there is still that category of "superstars" who are recognized. Jabez, as far as I know there are no supersaints. If there are, please respond immediately and correct me. Every Christian is a saint because of our participation in the holiness of Jesus Christ. Again, supersaints belong to the mentality of pre-Vatican II Roman Catholicism.

Another success story is told. Oh, Jabez, I'm getting tired of criticizing all of those success stories. I am happy for every person that is helped in finding the forgiveness and freedom that God gives through Jesus Christ. I'm delighted for everyone who has the privilege of helping one find that new life in Christ. I'm just tired of success stories, Jabez. I've said enough about them earlier. I haven't changed my mind.

UPWARD SPIRAL

Is there a "cycle of blessing," that results in "exponential growth"? Does one spiral "ever outward and upward"? I don't know, Jabez, and I don't really care. Oh, I don't mean that I am apathetic about my life with God. I care deeply. But this "upward spiral" has a hollow ring to it. I rather expect that faithfulness to God, serving others, fighting for the oppressed and disadvantaged, rather than producing an "upward spiral" may indeed lead to a downward spiral into suffering and even death. That was the spiral of Jesus' ministry.

We have the opportunity to read of that downward spiral, Jabez, an opportunity that you did not have. Perhaps you witnessed the whole scene from afar. As you know, it was only after the downward spiral of suffering and death that God raised Jesus from the dead, exalted him, and gave him a name that is above every name. I read about that humiliation, suffering, death, and subsequent exaltation in Paul's letter to the Philippians, chapter 2, verses

5-11. I quoted part of it earlier, but it is so beautiful that it is worth repeating. "Have this mind among yourselves, which is yours in Christ Jesus, who though he was in the form of God, did not count equality with God a thing to be grasped, but emptied himself, taking the form of a servant, being born in the likeness of men. And being found in human form he humbled himself and became obedient unto death, even death on a cross. Therefore God has highly exalted him and bestowed on him the name which is above every name, that at the name of Jesus every knee should bow, in heaven and on earth and under the earth, and every tongue confess that Jesus Christ is Lord, to the glory of God the Father." Isn't that grand, Jabez?

It seems to me that the author of the book about your prayer wants the exaltation without the humiliation, the upward spiral without the downward spiral, the glory without the cross. Indeed, the whole book smacks of a theology of glory rather than a theology of the cross. (Ask Martin Luther about that. He spoke passionately about the fundamental distinction in the way that the Christian faith is presented).

AGAIN, IT'S UP TO ME

Finally this, Jabez. "You will know beyond doubt that God has opened heaven's storehouse *because you prayed.*" My goodness! Because I prayed? Again, it is all up to me. Where did this self-centered religion come from? You know as well as I, Jabez. The Evil One wants it all to depend upon me—or you.

Jabez, I would never ask anyone to pattern their prayer life after mine—or yours. No! Never! Not because I prayed for it; only because of God's great loving kindness toward me. I will tell you again, such loving kindness elicits from me a spirit of worship.

A long time ago I learned from Martin Luther words that I have committed to memory—words so different from what I read in this book about your prayer, so much more profound, and so much more in tune with the tenor of the whole Bible. I'd like to share them with you.

> I believe that God has created me
>> and all that exists.
> He has given me and still preserves my body
>> and soul with all their powers.
> He provides me with food and clothing,
>> home and family, daily work, and all
>> I need from day to day.
> God also protects me in time of danger
>> and guards me from every evil.
> All this he does out of fatherly and divine
>> goodness and mercy, though I do not
>> deserve it.
> Therefore I surely ought to thank and praise,
>> serve and obey him.
> This is most certainly true.

I believe that Jesus Christ—true God,
    Son of the Father from eternity,
and true man, born of the Virgin Mary—
    is my Lord.
At great cost
he has saved and redeemed me,
a lost and condemned person.
He has freed me
from sin, death, and the power of the devil—
not with silver or gold,
but with his holy and precious blood
and his innocent suffering and death.
All this he has done that I may be his own,
live under him in his kingdom,
and serve him in everlasting righteousness,
    innocence, and blessedness,
just as he is risen from the dead and
lives and rules eternally.
This is most certainly true.

I believe that I cannot by my own
	understanding or effort
believe in Jesus Christ my Lord,
	or come to him.
But the Holy Spirit has called me
	through the Gospel,
enlightened me with his gifts,
and sanctified and kept me in the true faith.
In the same way he calls, gathers, enlightens,
	and sanctifies
the whole Christian church on earth,
and keeps it united with Jesus Christ
	in the one true faith.
In this Christian church day after day
he fully forgives my sins
and the sins of all believers.
On the last day he will raise me
	and all the dead
and give me and all believers in Christ
	eternal life.
This is most certainly true.

No, Jabez, it's not because I prayed or did anything else. I shall not say more lest I spoil what I learned from Martin Luther.

CHAPTER SEVEN

"SO GOD GRANTED HIM WHAT HE REQUESTED."

A PLAN

The last chapter of the book begins with a "plan." We are enjoined to read your prayer every day for a month, read the book once each week, and keep a record of changes in life that can be directly related to your prayer.

Jabez, I can speak for no one but myself, but I am very leery of my analytical ability. I fear that I would try to associate every event in my life with that prayer if I followed the guidelines of the suggested program. I would become a "believer." However, I would be seduced into becoming a believer *in your prayer*. I would believe that the prayer "worked." But my focus would be misplaced. Rather than worshiping and serving the God who has saved me from myself I would be focused and attentive to a prayer that "worked" and brought me great blessings. My basic self-centered desire to get more would be wonderfully satisfied.

It all centers in what I do. Listen to this. "It's only what you believe will happen *and therefore do next* that will release God's power for you and bring about a life change." Here we have a mixture of the power of positive thinking ("It's only what you believe will happen") and personal effort ("you . . . therefore do next").

There is a good bit of truth in the statement—believe strongly and work hard and you will reach your goals ("be blessed" in religious language). There is nothing in that statement that is anything more than a good bit of secular advice. It has nothing to do with our trust in God and our reliance on him to win the victory over evil for us, and accomplish his purpose through us, often without our knowledge. Not in believing hard and working hard, but in simple trust and hope we can say at the end of each day, for every failure, forgive us our trespasses, and for every victory, *Sola Deo Gloria*—to God alone be the glory!

Jabez, this emphasis on success is repeated again and again in the book about your prayer. It cannot be an accident but truly represents and reflects the popular religious secularism that is rampant in our world today.

GOD NEEDS HELP?

Another success story is told. It is evidence, according to the author, of what "God's grace and Jabez praying can do." God and me working together can do great things? It's too bad that God's grace alone is not sufficient, but must be accompanied by your prayer to be effective.

Jabez, I can't take the time to explain it to you but we have a phenomenon in my day—perhaps about eighty years old now—called Fundamentalism. For may years I have been amazed at how similar Fundamentalism is to Roman Catholicism prior to Vatican II, or even prior to the Reformation led by Martin Luther. Both talk a great deal about the grace of God, but both include works that the individual must do. To be sure, the specific works are different in each case, but grace *and* works, faith *and* works, are the signature of both.

The Christian tradition to which I belong clings tenaciously to the great themes of the Reformation: Grace Alone! Faith Alone! The Word of God Alone!

"God's grace and Jabez praying"? Never! God's grace alone is sufficient. When it is God's grace and my action, even the action of prayer, God and I can walk side by side as companions in victory; but when it is God's grace alone that accomplishes the victory, even though I may be an instrument that he uses, I can do nothing other than fall in worship before him.

REACHING THE WORLD FOR GOD

The one who wrote the book about your prayer has a great goal—to reach the whole world for God. Some may offer a sophisticated, patronizing smile; not I. I pray that his goal may be realized. If God has called him to that high noble task I applaud him, pray God's blessing on his efforts, and offer myself to God in the same service if that is where he chooses to use me. But in my support of the effort I pray that God will send me or someone more capable than I right behind to clean up the baloney that may be peddled—the baloney of cooperation between God and the individual, the baloney of seeking success in this life, the baloney that my prayer should be patterned after someone else's prayer.

Jabez, you can see that I have been very critical of the book written about your prayer. Unless convinced by Scripture or clear reason, I stand by my criticism. Yet I recognize my fallibility. Talk to

Peter and Paul, Martin Luther and John Calvin, the Wesley brothers, and others of that great cloud of witnesses that have preceded me and my contemporaries in this journey of massive ignorance with little, but sufficient light. Let me know where I have erred.

If other Believers should get a hold of this letter, I hope that they will grapple with the issues raised herein, and, under the guidance of God's Spirit find that life of forgiveness, freedom, and joy that leads always to worship and service.

Because I have been so critical (some may even label my letter as negative), I want to end on a positive note. I concur with the author of that other book when, within a page of the end of the book he says, "We are only weak humans who seek to be clean and fully surrendered to our Lord, to want what He wants for His world, and to step forward in His power and protection to see it happen now." I object only to the timing: "now." I shall leave the timing to God.

Thanks for taking the time to read such a long letter, Jabez. Oh well, I guess time means nothing to you.

Yours in a common Lord,

Neal E. Snider

P.S. Jabez, I have quoted from a book about your prayer. I am sure that it is of no interest to you but others who read this letter may want to know the publisher of the book. I'll include it here:

Wilkinson, Bruce H. *The Prayer of Jabez* (Sisters, Ore.: Multnomah Publishers, Inc., 2000).

I have also quoted Martin Luther's meaning to the three articles of the Apostles' Creed. There are many translations of those great words. The one that I used is from the following:

The Small Catechism by Martin Luther in Contemporary English (Copyright © 1960, 1968 Augsburg Publishing House, Board of Publication of the Lutheran Church in America, Concordia Publishing House).